JE

HELEN LESTER

TACKY *in* TROUBLE

Illustrated by LYNN MUNSINGER

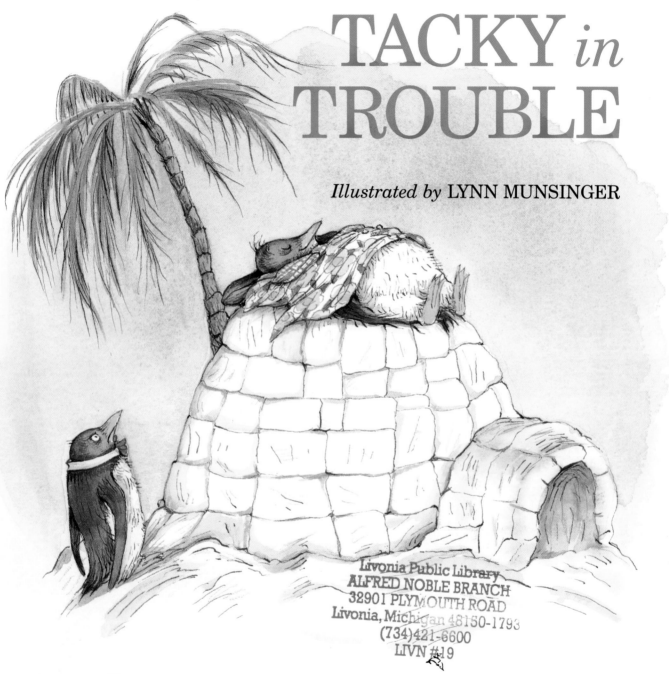

HOUGHTON MIFFLIN COMPANY BOSTON

For my son Robin —
always a nice bird to have around — H.L.

Walter Lorraine (un) Books

Text copyright © 1998 by Helen Lester
Illustrations copyright © 1998 by Lynn Munsinger

www.houghtonmifflinbooks.com

Library of Congress Cataloging-in-Publication Data
Lester, Helen.
   Tacky in trouble / by Helen Lester ; illustrated by Lynn
Munsinger
      p.   cm.
   Summary: Tacky the exuberant penguin accidentally goes
sailboarding and winds up on a tropical island, where he meets an
elephant who demands proof of Tacky's identity.
   RNF ISBN 0-395-86113-6 PA ISBN 0-618-38008-6
   [1. Penguins—Fiction. 2. Elephants—Fiction.] I. Munsinger,
Lynn, ill. II. Title.
PZ7.L56285Tab   1998
[E]—dc21   97-442
                                                                    CIP
                                                                    AC

RNF ISBN-13: 978-0-395-86113-4
PA ISBN–13:   978-0-618-38008-4

Manufactured in China
SCP   15   14   13   12   11

As Goodly, Lovely, Angel, Neatly, and Perfect sang
"Sunrise on the Iceberg," the sun rose on the iceberg.
They felt very much in charge.

"WHAT'S HAPPENING?" blared Tacky the penguin, greeting
each of his companions with a hearty slap on the back.
After breakfast the penguins went about their morning activities.

Whether they were ice-block building, napkin folding,
feather combing, or ballroom dancing, Tacky was the odd bird.
Then it was naptime. Naptime for all, that is, but Tacky.

"What a great day for surfing!" he cried.
"Would that be fun or what!"
"It would be what," said Goodly, Lovely, Angel,
 Neatly, and Perfect.
"Go surfing if you must, but please do it quietly."
 So Tacky took off alone and coasted over the waves.

Suddenly the wind came up, filling his shirt like a sail,
and he found himself blowing full speed ahead out to sea.
He loved the spray on his beak and the thrill of the ride.

On he sailed. And on and on, through sunny days
and starlit nights.
By the time he finally reached land he was
standing on tippy-webs on an ice cube.
With his little heart beating in excitement
Tacky waddled ashore, ready for an adventure.

After being greeted by the strangest
penguins he'd ever seen, he came
upon a large gray rock.
How nice. He had lots of rocks at home.
"Funny," thought Tacky. "This rock is warm."
The rocks he knew were cold.
"And it's a little squishy."
The rocks he knew were hard.
"And sort of hairy." Hairy?
He couldn't remember any hairy rocks
back on the iceberg.

Tacky never could sit still for long, so he did the little rock-hopping dance he'd always enjoyed doing at home.

I don't need shoes,
And I don't need socks,
Just my mellow yellow feet
for hopping on the rocks. HEY!

I don't need shoes,
And I don't need socks,
Just my mellow yellow feet
for hopping on the rocks. HEY!

I don't –

Suddenly the rock rose up and a voice louder than
any penguin's, a voice louder than even Tacky's, boomed
"SOMETHING IS TICKLING MY BACK."
Before Tacky could ask "What's happening?" the rock,
whose name happened to be Rocky, grabbed him,
and they were crashing through the jungle.

Tacky loved adventures, but was this fun or what?
He wasn't sure.
Finally Rocky came to a very gray clearing,
plunked Tacky down, and bellowed,
"FLOWERS FOR MY TABLE!"
While Tacky was puzzled, Rocky was overjoyed,
for she had taken one look at Tacky's shirt
and was convinced she had brought home the most
beautiful bunch of flowers in the world.
"Yes indeedy, just what I needed to brighten up
this dreary old place. Let's see, I'll need a
wide vase. It's a gorgeous bunch of flowers,
but pretty thick around the stem area."

After choosing her widest vase, Rocky plopped
Tacky in, and he looked around. The table
was set for dinner, with catsup and lemon pie and
grape punch and gravy and mustard and marmalade
and peanut butter and lots of other good things.
Rocky galumphed gleefully around the table singing,

Flowers make all the difference
Flowers make all the difference

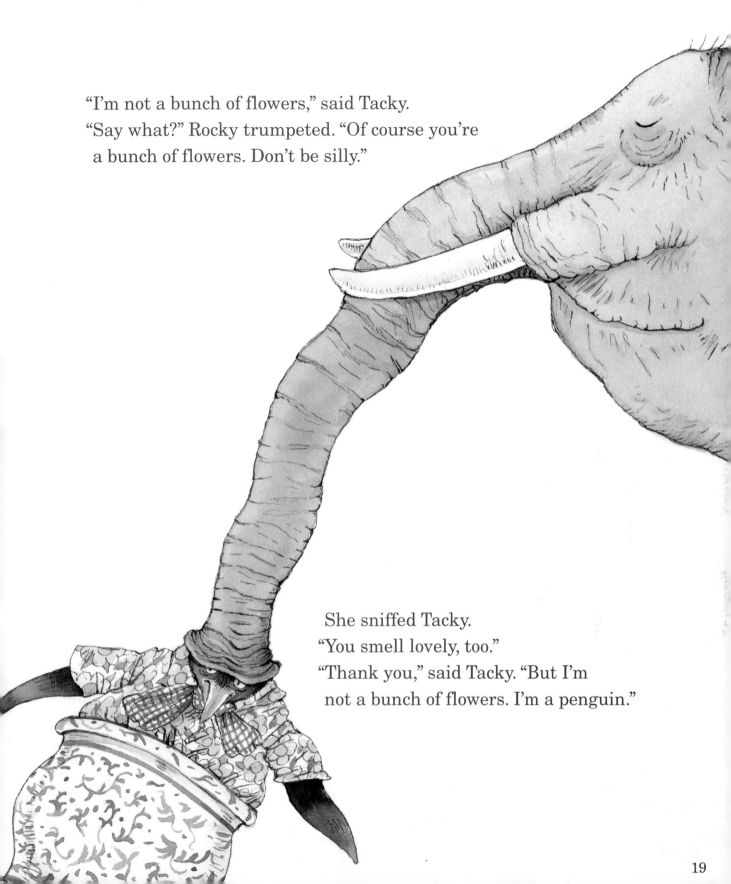

"I'm not a bunch of flowers," said Tacky.
"Say what?" Rocky trumpeted. "Of course you're
a bunch of flowers. Don't be silly."

She sniffed Tacky.
"You smell lovely, too."
"Thank you," said Tacky. "But I'm
not a bunch of flowers. I'm a penguin."

Rocky eyed Tacky suspiciously. "What's a penguin, some sort of weird plant?"

"No," offered Tacky, "it's a kind of bird."

"A bird!" snorted Rocky. "What a hoot! You're not like any bird *I've* ever seen."

Tacky felt his neck feathers prickle uncomfortably. "I'm really, honestly, truly a penguin," he repeated.

Rocky did not want to hear this.
She wanted flowers.
She *needed* those flowers, and her dull gray home
needed those flowers.
"If you're a penguin, prove it," Rocky demanded.
Then she reached out – whoosh – she snatched Tacky's shirt!
"At least I'm keeping the pretty blossoms, no matter
what. Well, unless you can convince me you're a penguin."
Tacky knew he was in trouble now. His shirt was his sail.
And without his shirt, how would he get home?
Would he ever see Goodly, Lovely, Angel, Neatly,
and Perfect again?

"Hurry up now. I'm hungry
and I don't have all day," snapped
Rocky impatiently. "Prove you're a
penguin. Do something penguinish."
Tacky thought very hard. He just
had to show her. "Oh yes," he
remembered. "Penguins march."

He began, 1, 2, 3 . . . *stepped* in the catsup bowl
without knowing it . . . and continued marching over the
table . . . 4, 5, 17, 100. "What else?" asked Rocky.

"Penguins belly-slide."

Tacky got a running start, skidded across the lemon pie, and swished in swirls over the tablecloth.

Mmmm. Where was that lemon smell coming from?

"Go on," ordered Rocky.

"Penguins dive."

Tacky took a bounding leap up and did a splashy cannonball into the pitcher of grape punch. Refreshing!

More confused than convinced, Rocky asked,

"And . . . ? Keep going."

What else? What else could a penguin do?
Then he remembered what had gotten him
into this situation in the first place, and he said,
"Penguins are excellent hoppers." Bravely
tilting his beak up in his best proper hopping form,
    he hopped in the gravy
    and hopped on the cloth

and hopped in the mustard
and hopped on the cloth
and hopped in the marmalade
and hopped on the cloth
and hopped . . . in . . . the peanut butter . . .
annnnd . . . stopped.

Then he waddled stickily over to Rocky.
"See?" he shrugged hopefully. "I'm a penguin."
Rocky looked at her red, yellow, purple, brown,
gold, orange, and tan tablecloth and bellowed,
"What have you done to my tablecloth?"
Tacky froze. He had been having fun doing
Penguin things, and hadn't even realized
that he'd made a mess.
"Uh oh," he thought. "I'm stuck here forever.
I'll never get home to my iceberg."

"My tablecloth! My tablecloth!" hooted Rocky.
"I love it, I simply love it!
 Look at those colors! They're brilliant!
 They're beautiful! And they're so much prettier than

your blossoms! No offense. Here you go, you wonderful,
odd whatever-you-are."
With that she picked up Tacky's shirt and flipped it to him.
She also threw him a hot dog, a cookie, and three kisses.
"THANK YOU!" she trumpeted as Tacky waved good-bye
and set out for the water's edge.

He leapt onto a log, thinking, "I didn't know ice blocks came
in brown," and as his shirt caught the wind he set sail.
Meanwhile, back on the iceberg, Goodly, Lovely, Angel, Neatly,
and Perfect were singing "Sunrise on the Iceberg." The sun rose,
but they didn't feel in charge. Life just hadn't been the same
without Tacky. Everything was so orderly, and they were tired of
patting each other on the back and whispering,
"What is happening?"
Nothing was happening.

Then they saw the speck in the distance. Could it be?
As the speck came closer and closer they could see it was Tacky!
Goodly, Lovely, Angel, Neatly, and Perfect hugged Tacky.
Tacky was an odd bird, but a nice bird to have around.

And many miles away an elephant sat by her colorful
tablecloth and thought the same thing.